This book
belongs to
name REBECCA
FROM GRANNY WITH LOVE
xx
XMAS 1987.

£3.50

bertha

1 "Atishoo! Excuse me!" sniffled Ted, sneezing for the fifth time that day. "You have a cold," said Mrs Tupp.

2 "What you need is a nice hot cup of tea. Then go straight home to bed." "Okay. Good idea," agreed Ted.

3 Next day, Miss McClackerty looked worried. "Mrs Tupp has rung to say she has Ted's cold. No tea today!"

4 "Wait! I have an idea," said Mr Willmake. "I know someone who could help us while Mrs Tupp is ill."

5 At tea-break, Mr Willmake's friend arrived. "I don't have tea, but would anyone like ice-cream?" he called.

6 "How funny," laughed Roy. "When Mrs Tupp catches a cold, we have cold ice-creams instead of hot tea!"

Henry's Cat and friends

1 Henry's Cat had entered a tug of war. He called his team 'Henry's Cat and friends', and began training.

2 Henry's Cat and friends trained every day for two weeks.. "I hope it is worth it," groaned Chris Rabbit.

3 "I can't do this," panted Mosey Mouse, trying his hardest. "I'm not Muscley Mouse, you know."

4 On the big day, Henry's Cat and friends won the first round easily. "How strong!" gasped the losers.

5 But Henry's Cat sighed when he saw the other finalist. "We don't stand a chance of winning against Myrtle!"

6 "But we can't lose," said Pansy. "Myrtle is a friend. Hooray for Henry's Cat and all his friends!"

1 It was nearly Christmas, but all was not well at the airport. "Where's the Christmas tree, Chief?" asked Jimbo.

2 "I forgot it," admitted the Chief. "And now it's too late. The shops have sold out. I can't find one anywhere."

3 "But the airport chef is making lots of Christmas puddings," he said, trying to cheer everybody up. It didn't work.

4 Jimbo had to fly people to Norway for a Christmas holiday. "They will have a Christmas tree," he sighed.

5 "What is the matter, Jimbo?" asked the Chief at Oslo airport, when he saw Jimbo sulking. Jimbo told him.

6 "But Norway has thousands of Christmas trees," said the Oslo Chief. "Take one back as a present."

7 "I can?" grinned Jimbo. "Gosh, thank you." A special tree was loaded before Jimbo took off for London.

8 Back home, everybody was very pleased with the tree. "How can we thank the Chief at Oslo?" they said.

9 "We ought to give Oslo airport a present," said Tommy. "What could we send?" Jimbo had an idea.

10 Jimbo flew to Oslo the next day. "Back already?" said the Chief. "This is a special trip," smiled Jimbo.

11 "This pudding is a present for you and the airport staff," said Jimbo. "From all of us at London Airport!"

MOP AND SMIFF

1 Mop and Smiff were in the park. Smiff had just sat down, while Mop chased a football, when three dogs started to chase her.

2 Smiff ran until she had found Mop. "Hello, Caeser, Oliver, Ben," smiled Mop. "I haven't seen you for ages." The dogs forgot Smiff.

3 On the way home, Smiff called on one of her friends. As Mop waited for her, he smiled at two cats on the wall. But they just hissed.

4 Mop was upset. As Smiff waved goodbye to her friend, the cats jumped down off the wall to chat with their old friend, Smiff.

© Mike Amatt 1987 Licensed by BBC Enterprises Ltd.

5 "I was only trying to be friendly, but your friends didn't like me," sighed Mop, walking home. "Your friends didn't like me, either," sighed Smiff.

6 "How silly! They probably think that cats and dogs have to be enemies!" laughed Mop. "What an unusual pair of friends we must be, Smiff!"

Smiff's sugar mice!

Makes eight mice

You will need:
1lb icing sugar
1 egg white
2oz golden syrup
a few drops of pink colouring
silver balls or chocolate chips
liquorice laces
almond flakes

This is what you do:
Sift the icing sugar into a bowl. Lightly beat the egg white in a separate bowl. Add the golden syrup and half of the icing sugar to the egg white and mix well. Gradually mix in the remaining icing sugar and knead with your hands into a smooth dough. Add the pink colouring and roll out the dough into a sausage shape. Divide the sausage into eight pieces and mould each piece into a mouse shape. Put in two almond flakes for ears, a liquorice lace for a tail and silver balls or chocolate chips for eyes. Eat your mice before they run away!

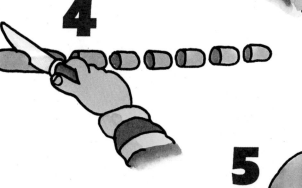

Jackson

written by Penny Johnson **illustrated by Chris Duggan**

"My life is so dull and boring!" complained Jackson, the black umbrella. "I'm always rolled up, upside down and all I ever see are feet and legs."

Jackson belonged to a gentleman who travelled up to London every day on the train. His owner had to go a short distance on foot to the office and, during that time, it never seemed to rain. Jackson felt more like a walking stick than an umbrella. He longed to be opened out and have a good soaking, the right way up!

Then, one morning, when Jackson and his owner were walking along the street, the sky suddenly became very dark. Then... *pitter, patter, plop! Splish, splash, splosh!* Down came the rain and it did not stop! It poured and poured.

"At last," said Jackson, as he felt himself being opened up.

"How glorious," he cried, stretching himself out to the full, to let the rain trickle down.

Just then, a gust of wind blew him right out of the gentleman's hand. Jackson found himself going along at a terrifying speed and climbing higher and higher. He flew over shops and theatres, red buses and trains. He whizzed past Buckingham Palace and only just missed Big Ben.

"Look at that umbrella!" people called out. But nobody could catch him. On and on Jackson went until the wind dropped and... clump!

"Wherever am I?" wondered Jackson, feeling rather shaky.

He paused for a moment. Then he looked down and saw grass, bright flowers, ducks on a lake and children playing. Jackson had become hooked on to a branch of a tree in Hyde Park.

"Now this is much more interesting than watching people's feet and legs in the city streets!" grinned Jackson. "I prefer it here."

And there he stayed.

Pigeon Street

1 A man from the council is painting black and white stripes across Pigeon Street. The pigeons are puzzled. They think it is strange.

4 Bob stops his bike when Daisy steps on the stripes. The pigeon is surprised. People usually stop for cars, not cars for people!

5 The pigeon calls its friends over. Mr Jupiter comes along. "About time we had one of these," he says. "Safest way to cross the road."

2 When the paint is dry, Mrs Glossop and the twins walk across the stripy pattern. "No cars are coming so we can cross safely," she says.

3 William crosses next. "Careful!" coos a pigeon on top of the new light. But Clara stops before the stripes and smiles at William.

6 The pigeons decide to test it for themselves. They wait on the kerb for a car to stop, then hop on the stripes to cross the road.

7 Mr Baskerville arrives with Watson. "I thought a stripy crossing was a zebra crossing," he smiles. "Now I shall call it a pigeon crossing!"

Hazel nut

In the autumn, hazel nuts can be found along many hedgerows in Britain. As well as being a favourite food for squirrels and mice, they are collected and sold in the shops for us. They are also known as cob nuts or as filberts, after an ancient saint. In the olden days, instead of throwing rice or confetti after a wedding, people threw hazel nuts at the bride and groom to bring good luck! Country folk used to think it very unlucky to pick hazel nuts on a Sunday. Some people used to believe keeping a hazel nut in your pocket would stop aches and pains.

Lucky or Unlucky?

Many people believe that certain things are lucky or unlucky. Have you ever heard of any of these superstitions?

It is unlucky to see a single magpie. If you do, you should salute it, saying, Good morning (or Good afternoon), Mr Magpie!
On the other hand, it is thought very lucky if you see two magpies.

Hanging a horseshoe above your front door is supposed to bring good luck to your house. But make sure it is hung like a 'u' so the good luck cannot fall out of it!

Make sure you walk around any ladders and not underneath them. Walking underneath a ladder is unlucky!

Finding a four-leafed clover is very lucky...and very unusual!

Many people believe that the number thirteen is unlucky, and that Friday 13th is especially unlucky. So be warned!

It is unlucky to put new shoes on a table!

It is lucky if a black cat crosses your path!

If you spill some salt, you should throw a pinch of salt over your left shoulder to avoid bad luck!

KING ROLLO *feels unwell*

1 One day, King Rollo woke up with a headache, a runny nose and a sore throat. "I have a cold!"

2 Cook felt his forehead. It was hot. "You have a temperature. I'll fetch you a cool drink," she said, kindly.

3 The Magician brought some fresh fruit. "Fruit is good for you," he said. Hamlet wanted some, too.

4 Queen Gwen came to visit him, bringing some special medicine made from honey and lemon.

King Rollo © 1987 David McKee.

5 Everyone wanted to look after King Rollo. They came to sit with him to keep him company while he was ill.

6 Soon he was feeling better. But everyone else had his cold! "I'll look after them now!" he said.

A snowman visits the Flumps

1 The Flumps were expecting Uncle Filbert to pay them a visit. But it was very cold out and snow was falling.

2 "Oh, dear," said Father. "I hope Uncle Filbert manages to find us. He could lose his way in the snow."

3 But Uncle Filbert was not lost. He was trudging through the snow and remembering his snowy adventures.

4 "I thought I'd found that beast, the Abominable Snowman. But it had a carrot nose and coal eyes!"

5 Father was still worrying when there was a knock at the door. He opened it and there stood a snowman.

6 "Help!" he cried, hiding. "Don't worry," laughed Posey. "I think the Abominable Uncle Filbert is here!"

Mop and Smiff masks

Carefully trace these outlines on to thin card. Colour your masks. Ask a grown-up to help you cut out the eye holes and around the dotted lines to make a flap for your nose to fit through. Poke small holes on either side of the masks and knot string or elastic through them to tie at the back of your head. You could play Mop and Smiff games with a friend.

© Mike Amatt 1987 Licensed by BBC Enterprises Ltd.

Postman Pat

To Postman Pat
Greendale
LA21 8ZX

1 One day, when Pat went to collect the letters from Mrs Goggins at the Post Office, there was a very strange-shaped parcel waiting to be delivered, too.

2 Mrs Goggins carefully lifted it over the counter and gave it to Pat. "I wonder what it can be?" she said.

GREENDALE

3 "Well, I wonder who it is for?" said Pat. "The label is smudged and I can't read the name or address."

4 Pat put the mystery parcel in his van and set off. "I'll ask everyone if it is for them," he told Jess.

5 Pat's first call was at Thompson Ground. "Is this your parcel?" he asked Alf. "It's not mine," said Alf.

6 Pat went to see Mrs Pottage next. "Is this for you?" he asked her. "I've not sent off for anything," she replied.

7 Pat called at Sam Waldron's mobile shop. "Could this be your parcel?" Sam shook his head.

8 But then Sam had a thought. He shouted after Pat, "Try Ted Glen. He orders strange things sometimes!"

9 But the parcel wasn't Ted's, either. "Why not open it and have a look. That might give you a clue."

10 "That is a very good idea," said Pat. He tore the wrapper off. "What on earth is it?" asked Ted.

11 Pat felt very silly. "This parcel is for me!" he laughed. "It's the watering-can I ordered!"

you and me

Richard is helping his dad in the garden.

They are sowing vegetable seeds.

Richard sows the seeds in rows. Can you see the length of string? Richard is following it to make sure his rows are straight.

Dad rakes soil over the seeds. "I hope the birds don't eat these," he laughs.

Seeds like plenty of water.

Richard's dad has made signs to remind him which seeds he is growing in each row.

peas

carrots

lettuce

© BBC 1987.

It does not take long for the tiny seeds to shoot up as little green seedlings.

And in the summer, those little seedlings will be tasty vegetables for Richard and his family to eat.

Can you see what vegetables they have grown?

Have you ever grown anything?

Jimbo to the rescue

The Chief was in a very good mood. He had hardly shouted at anyone at all.

"Morning, everyone," he smiled, as he crossed the runway.

"The Chief is looking pleased with himself today," whispered Jimbo to Tommy Tow Truck.

The Chief overheard him.

"I'm going to be Best Man at my brother Stanley's wedding tomorrow," he grinned.

"I love weddings," sighed Amanda Baggage Truck.

"What does Best Man do?" asked Tommy.

"He helps the bridegroom," explained the Chief, "and looks after the wedding ring." He took a box from his pocket. Inside was a gold ring. "Stanley gave it to me to look after until tomorrow."

Amanda gave another sigh.

"How lovely!"

"I have to make a speech, too," said the Chief, putting the ring back in his uniform pocket before Amanda became too fond of it.

The next day, the Chief enjoyed showing off his suit to everyone.

"You look very smart, Chief," said his Assistant.

The Chief beamed with pleasure.

"Can you take my uniform to the cleaners?" he asked. "I might as well have it cleaned while I don't need it."

The Chief drove off to the wedding and his Assistant left for the cleaners. Jimbo, who had no flights that morning, watched them leave. But half an hour later, the Chief's Assistant came rushing back.

"The Chief forgot to take the wedding ring out of his uniform!" she cried. "The lady at the cleaners found it. You must fly it to the church, Jimbo," she said, giving Jimbo the little box. "Quickly, there's not a moment to lose!"

Jimbo took off straight away. He whizzed over the countryside and swooped down into a field next to the church — just as the Chief and his brother, Stanley, were about to go in.

"Wait!" Jimbo called. "You forgot the ring, Chief!"

"Oh, er thanks, Jimbo," said a very red-faced Chief. "That could have been most embarrassing!"

"You must stay for the wedding, Jimbo," invited Stanley. "Without your help, I could not have got married today."

So Jimbo was a very special guest at Stanley's wedding. Somebody even found him a top hat to wear!

Flying fish kite

Ask a grown-up to help you cut out the middle of a paper plate and use the outside rim as your fish's mouth. Tape a sheet of tissue paper to the mouth and join it as shown. Make slits at the end of the tissue paper, then fasten them together at the top of the slits to bunch the tassles you have made together like a tail. Make flowing scales and eyes from paper and stick them to your fish. Cover the mouth with silver foil. Carefully make two holes on either side of the mouth and knot the string through them. Run with your fish behind you to make it fly.

1 The valuables at Spottiswood's are kept in a safe in Mr Willmake's office. You need a code to open it.

2 One day, Mr Willmake could not remember the code. "Oh, dear," he sighed. "I'll have to cut it open!"

3 "Where can we put our money and valuable things in the meantime?" he worried. Mr Sprott had an idea.

4 "We'll ask Bertha to make another safe," he said. Soon a shiny new safe appeared on Bertha's chute.

5 "We have a safe, but we don't know its code!" sighed Roy. "It is as useless as Mr Willmake's one!"

6 Bertha started up again. "Bertha knows the code. I knew we would be *safe* with her!" laughed Ted.

Silent night, holy night.
All is calm, all is bright.

Jemima has made a Nativity scene.
You could make one, too.

Scatter shreds of yellow paper inside a box as straw. Wrap old toilet rolls with scraps of material to make bodies for your figures. Use cotton wool balls for their heads. Glue cotton wool around a cotton reel to make a sheep and give your sheep matchstick legs. Make the baby Jesus from a cotton reel and lay in a match box crib. Use small pieces of coloured paper and material to make faces for your figures, and to decorate the walls of your stable. You could make a window showing a starry night.

Little Ted is making starry decorations for the Play School Christmas tree. You could make some for your tree.

You need:
2oz butter
1oz sugar
3oz flour

Crumble the butter, sugar and flour together in a big mixing bowl until it looks like breadcrumbs. Add a few drops of milk and roll the crumbs into a ball. Roll out the ball on a floured board.

Ask a grown-up to help you carefully cut out star shapes and make a hole in the middle of each star. Then ask them to cook the stars in an oven at 350° F or Gas mark 4. When they are cool, you could decorate them with icing. Tie coloured ribbons through the holes in the middle.

Now hang your stars on your tree.

Henry's Cat and friends

1 "What a lovely dream," sighed Henry's Cat. "I dreamed I was eating mountains of food!"

2 The dream gave Henry's Cat an idea. "I will hold a competition. Whoever eats the most, wins."

3 He went to tell his friends. "I'm practising already," he told them, biting into a big piece of cake.

4 Everyone started collecting food. "I'm looking forward to this," said Douglas. "Me, too," said Pansy.

5 Henry's Cat and friends put the food in a pile. "Ready, steady, go!" shouted Henry's Cat. "Yum, yum!"

6 He was still eating at midnight. "I had better eat until morning," he said, "so the others see me win!"

Chris Rarebit!

When Henry's Cat invites his friend Chris Rabbit to tea, he likes to make Chris his favourite snack as a joke!

You will need:

½oz butter
2oz cheese
½ tablespoon milk
mustard, salt and pepper
1 slice bread

This is what you do:

Put the butter in a bowl and cream it with a wooden spoon until it is soft. Ask a grown-up to help you grate the cheese, then add the cheese, milk, and a little mustard, salt and pepper to the butter and stir well. Ask a grown-up to help you toast the bread, then spread the rarebit mixture on top of the toast. Grill the toast topped with rarebit under a hot grill for about four minutes or until the mixture is brown. Eat at once! Chris always does!

Henry's Cat likes this snack best with a sardine on top. You might like it, too.

The butterfly farm

Matthew's class had been painting butterflies at play school.

"We should take you to see some real butterflies and moths at the butterfly farm," said mum.

"Butterfly farm? There's no such thing," said Matthew, in disbelief.

"Oh, yes there is," smiled mum. "I'll ask dad if he wants to come with us at the weekend."

Matthew could not wait for the weekend to arrive. He had never visited a real farm before. But when they arrived at the butterfly farm, Matthew was surprised to find it was just a large house. There were no fields of animals to be seen anywhere. But inside the house, there were hundreds of butterflies flying all over the rooms.

"Why don't they live outside like other butterflies?" asked Matthew, curiously.

"These butterflies can only live outside in very hot countries," explained dad. "It's much too cold for them to be outside here."

written by Hilda Maudsley
illustrated by Alan Rogers

In one room in the house, were two large glass domes with big air holes. There were moths' eggs inside one. Some of the eggs had hatched and the silk worms were busy feeding on mulberry leaves. In the second dome, were tiny cocoons of silk thread which the silk worms spun around themselves before changing into fully-grown moths.

"When the silk worm has finished with the cocoon and it is empty," explained mum, "they are spun into silk for us."

Matthew was fascinated by the cocoons popping up and down as the thread was spun on to bobbins. Some of the silk had been made into scarves, dresses and lots of other pretty things.

"Aren't the silk worms clever!" exclaimed Matthew.

Mum, dad and Matthew went into another room.

"More butterflies!" said Matthew.

"No, these are moths," said dad.

"But they look just like butterflies," said Matthew, puzzled. "How do you know they are moths?"

"Can you see the tiny antennae sticking out of their heads?" asked dad, pointing at them.

Matthew looked closely. Yes, he could see them waving this way and that.

"Butterflies have little knobs on the ends of their antennae and moths don't," explained dad.

"Now I'll be able to paint pictures of butterflies and moths, and explain the difference to everyone at play school, too!" grinned Matthew. "And I think I'll call my picture, butterfly farm!"

KING ROLLO and the cards

1 The Magician was reading his old spell books. "Very interesting. I must try that one," he said to himself.

2 "I would like to do magic, too," said King Rollo. "Let's ask the Magician if he will teach me a spell."

3 But the Magician was horrified. "Only I can work magic spells!" King Rollo was disappointed.

4 "I could teach you some card tricks, though," said the Magician, kindly. He went to find a pack of cards.

5 "I have just made up a magic vanishing trick of my own," smiled King Rollo, climbing on to a chair.

6 He held up the cards. "Now you see a pack of cards." King Rollo dropped them. "Now you don't!"

King Rollo © 1987 David McKee.

It's magic!

The Magician taught King Rollo some real card tricks, too. You could try this one on your friends, but you may need to practise it first.

Shuffle a pack of cards and hold them so that they are facing downwards. Turn the card at the bottom of the pack up so that it is facing the rest of the cards.

Ask a friend to take a card from the pack without telling you what card it is. While your friend is looking at the card, secretly turn the pack over so that the bottom card is at the top. Because you had turned over the bottom card before starting the trick, your friend will not notice the pack looking any different. Ask your friend to replace his/her card face downwards in the pack so you cannot see it. Make sure you hold the pack tightly while the card is being replaced. You don't want your friend to see the cards are upside down!

Now turn away from your friend and pace up and down pretending to work out by magic what the card could be. As you do so, flick through the pack until you find your friend's card which will be facing the opposite way to all the others. Then magically announce what the card was.
Your friend will be amazed!

MOP AND SMIFF

1 It had snowed during the night. "I must tell Smiff," thought Mop. But she was not in her basket. "She must have gone out already!" said Mop.

2 "It's not like Smiff to go out without me," said Mop, feeling a bit hurt. "We always go together." But at the park, everything was quiet.

3 "Smiff!" called Mop. "Where are you?" Nobody answered. Then he saw paw prints in the snow. "They must be Smiff's," he grinned.

4 Mop put his head down and started to follow the paw print trail. Soon he found himself in his own road. "She must have gone home," he thought.

5 Smiff was in her basket. "You went out without me!" she yawned. "No, you went without me," said Mop. "I followed your prints home."

6 Smiff giggled. "You must have followed your own prints!" "Silly me!" blushed Mop. "I did think your paws looked rather large!"

Aunt Myrtle drops in for tea

1 It was a windy day. Aunt Myrtle was walking over the hills, humming. She was on her way to visit the Flumps.

2 She thought she felt rain in the air. "I hope I don't get blown away," she laughed, putting up her brolly.

3 Suddenly, a gust of wind blew and Aunt Myrtle sailed gently up into the air, still clutching on to her umbrella.

4 Aunt Myrtle thought she would be scared, but instead she felt excited, as she looked down at the world.

5 Suddenly, her brolly broke and she started to fall. "I hope I land on something soft," she cried.

6 She flew through the Flumps' open window and landed on Father. "I just dropped in for tea," she giggled.

Henry's Cat and friends

1 Henry's Cat decided to paint the constable's gate. "It could do with a coat of paint," he said.

2 Constable Bulldog arrived. "What's all this?" he frowned. "I don't like brightly-coloured gates."

3 "I have an idea," said Chris Rabbit. "Tip your pots of paint into this bucket." Everyone was puzzled.

4 But Henry's Cat saw what Chris was up to. He stirred the paints until he had made a sludgy colour.

5 "I can paint it without annoying the constable now," said Henry's Cat. "But I liked the red paint."

6 Chris handed Henry's Cat the red paint. "He didn't say anything about brightly-coloured words!"

Watch the birdie!

You can make birds from newspaper, paper bags, coloured paper and cardboard.

Draw a bird shape on a piece of card. Place it on top of another piece of card and cut out the bird. Bend back the wings and place a length of string between the two bird shapes. Glue the shapes together.

Scrunch up a ball of newspaper and put it in a paper bag, fastening the bag with sticky tape. Make fans of paper for your bird's wings and tail. Give your bird a paper beak and matchstick legs.

Around the world with Jimbo!

Make yourself a paper aeroplane. You may need to ask a grown-up to help you.

Take four sheets of newspaper and lay them on the floor.

Label each sheet with the name of a country.

Now try and fly your plane so that it lands on a country.

Each player takes it in turn to have four throws.

The first player to land in all four countries is the winner!

Over and out!

Jimbo has received a message over the radio, but the words have become mixed up. It should be a list of all the countries he has to visit. Can you help him sort them out?

ARIACF - - - - - -

ENDLNAG - - - - - - -

FECRAN - - - - - -

ILTYA - - - - -

SNPIA - - - - -

AACMEIR - - - - - - -

ANSWERS: Africa. England. France. Italy. America. Spain.

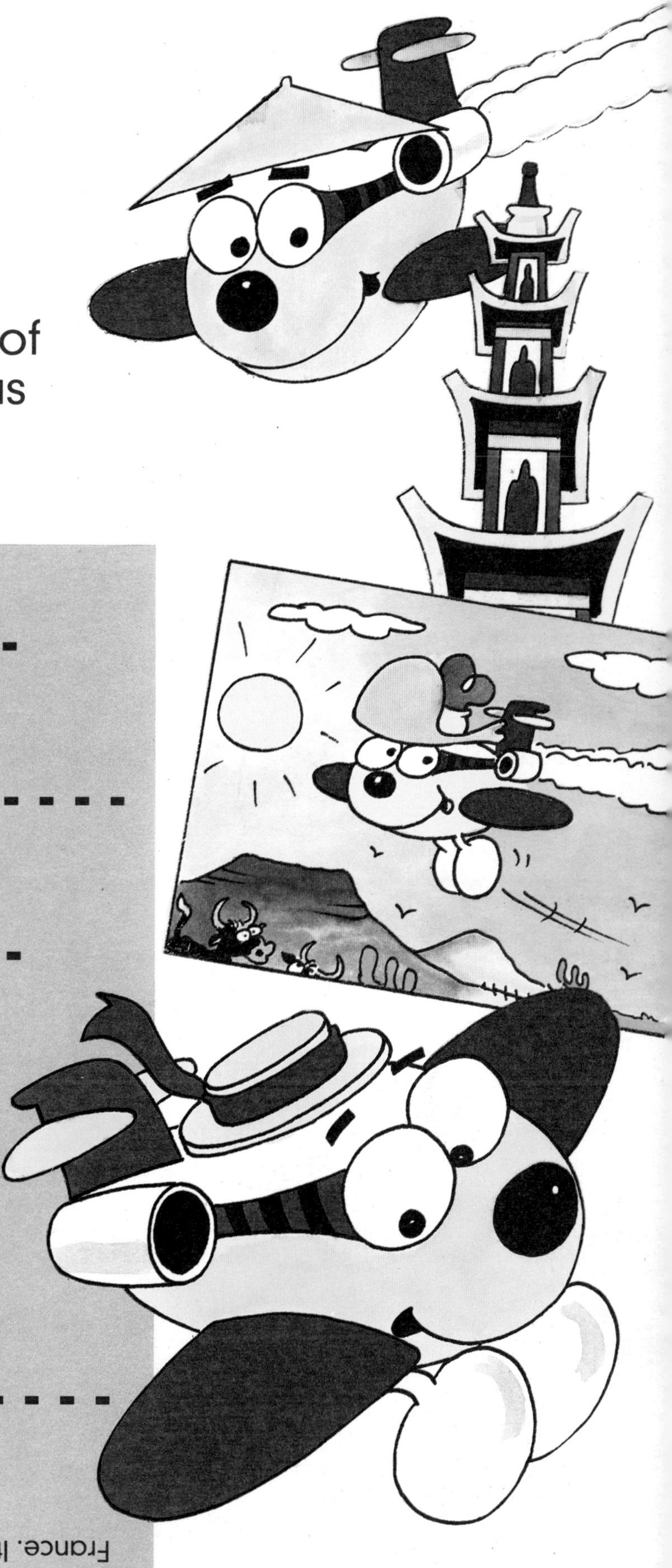

Pigeon Street

1 There is a bird sitting on a roof in Pigeon Street. But it is not a pigeon. This bird has escaped from the zoo.

2 The pigeons have never seen one quite like it before. "Coo!" they say. "Eeerch!" the bird screeches at them.

3 From the top floor of Skyrise Court, Mr Baskerville is the first to spot it. He telephones Mr Macadoo.

4 "It's from Africa," says Mr Macadoo. "It won't survive long in this cold weather. I'd better try to catch it."

5 But the bird flies off to the park where it lands next to Mrs Glossop. "Erch!" it says to Mrs Glossop's hat.

6 Mr Macadoo arrives and catches the bird. "It thinks you're a bird, too!" he chuckles. "Erch!" says Mrs Glossop.

Dragonfly

Dragonflies can look a bit frightening, but they are harmless. There are many different dragonflies in Britain. They begin life under water, spending two years as underwater nymphs before crawling up out of the water to hatch as adult dragonflies, with beautiful jewel-coloured bodies. Dragonflies have two large eyes made up of thousands of smaller eyes. In the early summer, you can often see dragonflies skimming ponds and rivers using those eyes to hunt small insects. Your eyes would have to be sharp to keep track of a dragonfly. They fly very fast!

1 After a very busy morning delivering the post in Greendale, Pat felt rather tired. He and Jess stopped by a lake to rest and look at the beautiful scenery.

2 As they were relaxing at the water's edge, a swan swam towards them. Jess went to have a closer look.

3 "Careful you don't get your feet wet," laughed Pat. "You don't like water." Jess just watched the swan.

4 "I think he wants something to eat," said Pat. "Shall I throw him some bread?" Jess looked worried.

5 Suddenly, the swan stood up out of the water, making a strange noise. "Hiss!" it went, beating its wings.

6 "Goodness!" cried Pat, jumping up. "Meow!" agreed Jess. The swan pecked at Pat's trouser legs.

7 Pat was so frightened, he ran to his van without picking up his bag or his sandwiches. "Quick, Jess!"

8 The swan stopped to nibble Pat's sandwich. It looked pleased with itself and fluffed up its feathers.

9 Pat, in the meantime, had bumped into Peter Fogg. "Help!" cried Pat. "There is a mad swan by the lake!"

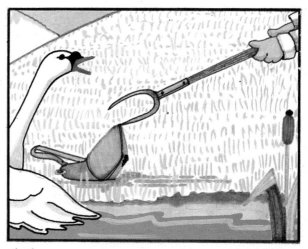

10 Peter went to the lake. "That swan isn't mad," he smiled. "It is looking after baby swans."

11 Peter used his hay fork to rescue Pat's bag. "I'll keep away from baby swans in future," said Pat.

Little Ted has planted spring flowers.
Can you name the flowers he is growing?
How many flowers do you think there will be altogether?

Growing with Little Ted

Flowers make a garden look colourful and bright. Why don't you colour in these flowers with Little Ted and make your own splash of colour.

"The pigeons of Pigeon Street are just passing by.
But watch out below — who's that we can spy?
That naughty cat, Tom, has a glint in his eye!
So, pigeons, stay safe and keep flying high!"

The pigeons in Pigeon Street are a bit like magpies.
They like to collect things. Can you find ten Happy
Buttons hidden in this picture?

The little star

"The star who shines the brightest at midnight, tonight, will be given something special," announced the chief star on Christmas Eve.

The stars began to argue straight away about which one had the brightest shine. But Tiny, the smallest star, said nothing at all.

"You've absolutely no chance of winning," sneered the biggest star.

"I suppose not," said Tiny.

He was watching the woodland animals stringing coloured lanterns from the trees.

"They are for our special visitor," they explained to Tiny. But it was beginning to snow quite heavily and a thick layer of snow covered everything.

"Oh, bother! The snow is covering the lanterns," grumbled the rabbits.

"It's all right. The stars are shining. We'll be able to see our visitor when he arrives," said the squirrels.

"Oh, no you won't," sniggered the biggest star. "We have to rest now, so we can shine our brightest at midnight."

"What are we going to do now?" groaned the rabbits. The squirrels and rabbits thought hard.

"Can't you help us, Tiny?" said one squirrel, after a while.

"I'm a bit small, but I'll do my best," said Tiny. And he shone as hard as he could.

Suddenly, they heard the sound of bells. Then a sleigh drawn by a reindeer landed in the snow.

"It's Santa Claus!" cried Tiny.

"Our visitor!" cried the woodland animals.

"I'm a bit early," beamed Santa. "Where are all the other stars?"

"They're resting," explained Tiny.

"Resting! I told the chief star to make sure they were all shining brightly. My new reindeer doesn't know the way here very well."

"They all want to win the special prize. That's why they're resting," snorted the rabbits.

"Ah yes, I did promise a prize for the brightest star," smiled Santa. "So why aren't you resting, too, little star?"

"I wanted to help my woodland friends," said Tiny, shyly. "They had no light to greet you."

"Well, I'm very grateful," chuckled Santa.

Tiny sparkled and shone with pride. When the other stars appeared, he was still twinkling away merrily.

Santa frowned sternly at the other stars, who looked ashamed when they saw who it was.

"I am awarding Tiny the special prize of a trip around the world on my sleigh tonight," he said. "Tiny will guide my reindeer because he is the brightest star of you all."

Tiny glowed with joy and, for once, the biggest star had nothing to say.

written by Pam Ramage
illustrated by Andy Ellis

Henry's Cat and friends

1 Henry's Cat had decided he wanted to be a film director. "I need to find a star to be in my film," he said.

2 "I need to take photos of you all to see which one of you would look best in my film," he told his friends.

3 He snapped Myrtle alone. "Am I a star?" she asked. "No, I just couldn't fit you in the other photo," he said.

4 "I look most like a star," boasted Pansy Pig. "Er, not with that funny feather scarf," said Henry's Cat.

5 "I look best from the side view," cried Chris, leaping over. "Hmm, not quite right," sighed Henry's Cat.

6 He called his friends outside. "I need a star more like me. What about Henry's Snow Cat Superstar!"

1 "Good morning, Bertha," said Ted. "We have a busy day today." Ted checked a hanger on her chute.

2 "I have a special job for you," Ted added. "You must work hard so Flo is busy packing all morning."

3 Bertha worked very fast. Flo and Nell were kept busy packing and stacking. "Phew!" puffed Nell.

4 Suddenly, Flo was alone. "Where is everyone?" she wondered. Ted sneaked away quietly.

5 "Surprise!" called Mrs Tupp. Flo turned around. "Happy Birthday, Flo!" everyone cried.

6 "That was fun," Ted said to Bertha. "Thanks for keeping Flo busy while we wrapped her presents!"

Pigeon Street

1 It is a stormy day in Pigeon Street. The sky is dark except for the flashes of lightning. CRASH goes the thunder. Watson does not like it.

4 "A storm can't hurt you," he smiles. "Just pretend the thunder is a piano falling down a wobbly lightning staircase. That's why it is so noisy!"

5 Watson begins to feel a bit better. When the thunder crashes again, he growls bravely back at it, barking loudly and wagging his tail.

2 In fact, he runs to hide from the storm. Mr Baskerville looks for Watson everywhere. He finds him under his bed. "Why are you hiding?" he asks.

3 But Watson just dashes off to hide somewhere safer. Mr Baskerville finds him in a cupboard. "Are you frightened of the storm?" he asks.

6 The storm begins to pass over. "What a fierce dog you are!" jokes Mr Baskerville. "You have scared that storm away!"

7 When they go outside, the sky is clear. "People will want to borrow you every time there's a storm!" he smiles. Watson wags his tail.

The new address

Pat climbed into his van.

"You will have to help me find it," he told Jess. Jess meowed back, trying to be helpful. They drove around the country lanes looking for April Farm until it was time for tea.

"Well, Jess," sighed Pat at last, "I think we will have to send this letter back to Head Office. Maybe they will be able to help us. Let's go and tell Mrs Goggins."

"I give up," admitted Pat, when he arrived at the Post Office. "I can't find April Farm anywhere."

But Mrs Goggins began to giggle.

"You are funny, Pat!" she laughed. "I wrote that envelope. Loof is fool spelt backwards. Didn't you remember that today is April fool's day. It was an April fool's joke!"

Pat blushed. "How silly I am!" he laughed.

"Good morning, Pat," said Mrs Goggins. "There are lots of letters and parcels for you to deliver today."

"Oh, good," smiled Pat. He enjoyed visiting all his friends around Greendale.

Mrs Goggins bent down behind the counter. "There's an address I don't think you've been to before," smiled Mrs Goggins. "Er, it's a Mr Loof of April Farm, Greendale. I think it's probably somewhere near Thompson Ground."

Pat looked puzzled. "April Farm? I've never heard of it. I thought I knew everywhere in Greendale. Oh, well, I shall just have to drive around and see if I can find it," he said.

Pat set off around Greendale delivering all the other letters and parcels first. One of his last deliveries was to Alf and Dorothy Thompson.

"Do you know where April Farm is?" he asked Dorothy, as he gave her a parcel.

"I've never heard of it," she replied, shaking her head.

There are seven differences between these two pictures of Pat and his friend, Peter Fogg. Can you spot them all?

answers: red letter, extra sheep, white-headed sheep, missing tree, missing puffs of smoke, square tractor wheel, missing tractor part.

1 "Whatever is the matter?" Jimbo asked a big jet. "There's a g-g-ghost at Raven airport," the jet stuttered.

2 Raven airport had been empty for years. It was an old wartime airfield. Jimbo laughed. "Don't be so silly!"

3 "I heard a ghost," the jet said, firmly. Jimbo and the Chief went to see. "I hope he's wrong," said the Chief.

4 But when they reached the airfield, they had a shock. WHOO! Spooky noises came from the old tower!

5 "It is haunted!" cried the Chief. "Get me out of here, Jimbo!" But as Jimbo flew away, he spotted somebody.

6 "Where's that paint which glows in the dark?" asked Jimbo, back home. "The stuff we use for airport signs."

7 "What's the idea of covering yourself with this?" said the puzzled Chief. "Wait and see," replied Jimbo.

8 "We are going haunting for ghosts," giggled Jimbo. "You mean hunting!" laughed the Chief, nervously.

9 "I mean haunting!" said Jimbo, swooping down to the tower, howling. "There go the ghosts!"

10 "A tape recorder!" said the Chief. "Those boys were playing ghost noises over the loudspeaker!"

11 "Now they've seen a ghost, I don't think they will be playing spooky games again," laughed Jimbo.

KING ROLLO *and the costume ball*

1 One day, King Rollo and Queen Gwen received an invitation to a fancy dress ball. "How exciting!"

2 "I shall go as a pirate," said King Rollo. "And I shall dress up as a beautiful fairy," said Queen Gwen.

3 "Shall we dance?" laughed King Rollo. "Your toy dagger sticks into me!" groaned the Magician.

4 "You can't wear that hat either. It knocks my star," said Queen Gwen. "But I need a hat!" said King Rollo.

5 Suddenly, King Rollo had an idea. "Take these away. I have a new costume," he said excitedly.

6 King Rollo decided to go as a clown. "Now instead of prickling people, I can tickle them!" he giggled.

MOP AND SMIFF

1 Smiff was hungry. "Let's play a game to take your mind off it," said Mop. "How about name your favourite food?" said Smiff.

2 "Hmm, I don't think so," said Mop. "We'll play hide and seek. I'll hide and you can find me." Smiff shut her eyes and began to count to ten.

3 Mop ran out to the garden. There was nowhere secret there. He peered in the hallway cupboard. But it was cluttered up with brooms.

4 Mop hurried into the sitting room and squeezed behind the sofa just in time. "Coming!" shouted Smiff. Mop tried not to make a sound.

5 Smiff scampered around the house. She crept into the sitting room last of all and spotted Mop. "Boo!" she shouted, squeezing in beside him.

6 "Are you still hungry?" asked Mop. "Yes," said Smiff. "Another name for this is squashed sardines! And I love sardines!"

Now you have nearly finished the annual, see how much you can remember of the stories. When you have filled in all the answers, a special word will be revealed.

1 His dog learnt not to be afraid of storms. He renamed a crossing in his street. What is his surname?

2 Aunt Myrtle's . . . took her flying. Another one landed in Hyde Park.

3 The caterpillar took you on one to find out about hazel nuts and dragonflies.

4 A Little one was digging his spring garden.

5 Jimbo found lots of Christmas trees at this airport.

6 On her friend's birthday, she was busy helping with the packing and stacking.

7 She was in her basket while her friend thought he was following her paw prints in the snow.

Cut out this page and cut along the thick black lines to make a jigsaw puzzle. You could stick this page to card first.